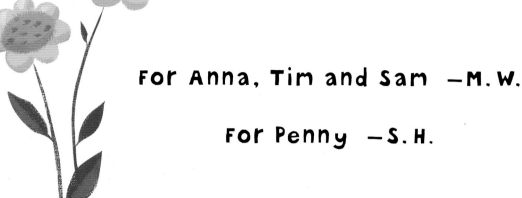

For Anna, Tim and Sam —M.W.

For Penny —S.H.

Text © 2003 by Marina Windsor.
Illustrations © 2003 by Steve Haskamp.

Book design by Jessica Dacher.
Typeset in Bokka and EideticNeo.
The illustrations in this book were rendered in acrylic.
Manufactured in Hong Kong.

Frisbee is a registered trademark of Wham-O, Inc.

Library of Congress Cataloging-in-Publication Data
Windsor, Marina.
Bad dog Max! / Marina Windsor ; illustrated by Steve Haskamp.
p. cm.
Summary: Everyone thinks that Max is a bad dog because she misbehaves,
until a veterinarian gives her owner a tip on how to make things better.
ISBN 0-8118-3700-9
[1. Dogs—Fiction. 2. Behavior—Fiction.] I. Haskamp, Steve, ill. II.
Title.
PZ7.W72445 Bad 2003
[E]—dc21
2002012367

Distributed in Canada by Raincoast Books
9050 Shaughnessy Street, Vancouver, British Columbia V6P 6E5

10 9 8 7 6 5 4 3 2 1

Chronicle Books LLC
85 Second Street, San Francisco, California 94105

www.chroniclekids.com

Bad Dog Max!

By Marina Windsor Illustrated by Steve Haskamp

chronicle books·san francisco

This is my dog, Max. Max gets into lots of trouble.

Sometimes my
mommy says,
"Bad dog, Max!"

Our cat, Monroe, thinks
Max is a bad dog.

Our neighbors think
Max is a bad dog.

My daddy said,
"**Bad dog, Max!**"
when she stole
our dinner.

The mailman thinks Max is very naughty. We had to move our mailbox because he wouldn't come into the yard anymore.

When my aunt came to
visit she didn't call Max bad,
she called her *dreadful.*

That's even
worse!

"No! Bad dog, Max!"
I said when she spilled
my cereal and milk.

Max makes
everybody mad!

One day Mommy and I took Max
to the vet for a checkup. The Vet said,
"I have a dog just like Max."

She explained that Max doesn't mean to be bad. She just has lots of energy. She told us to take Max on long walks and to play with her.

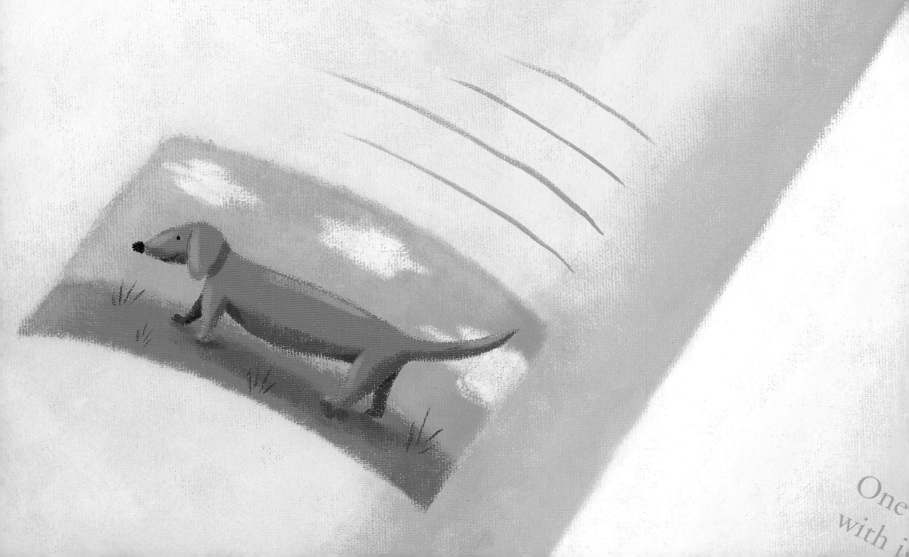

One with

Australian Cattle Dog

Very active breed. Likes to fetch. Requires lots of exercise. Likes long, vigorous walks at least twice a day. Perky, upright ears. Strong sense of smell. Very protective. Barks a lot.

Australian Ke...
...he sp...

Now Max loves going to
the park and playing with
her new dog friends. She has
a real talent for catching
a Frisbee.

GOOD catch, Max!

She still gets in trouble sometimes, but I love her just the way she is.

Good dog,
Max!

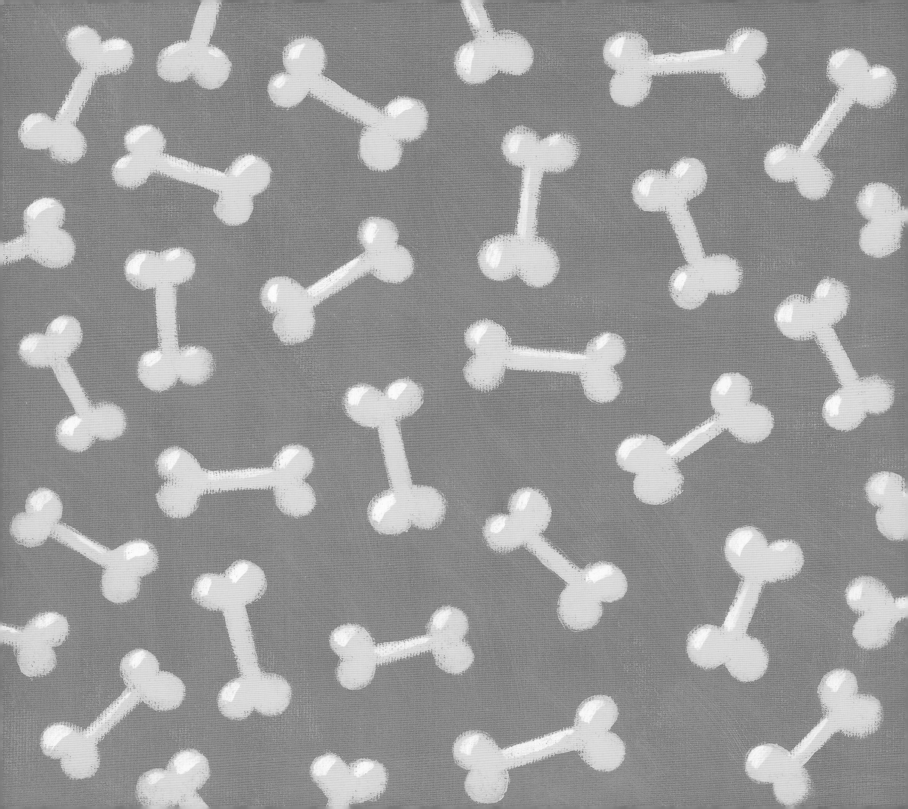